THE BOX WITH
RED WHEELS

THE BOX WITH RED WHEELS

A PICTURE BOOK

BY MAUD AND MISKA PETERSHAM

MACMILLAN PUBLISHING COMPANY
New York

COLLIER MACMILLAN PUBLISHERS
London

Macmillan Publishing Company, 866 Third Avenue, New York, NY 10022
Collier Macmillan Canada, Inc.
First published 1949; reissued 1986
Printed in the United States of America
10 9 8 7 6 5 4 3 2 1
The Library of Congress has cataloged the first printing of this title
as follows:
Petersham, Maud (Fuller) 1890 – 1971.
The box with red wheels, a picture book by Maud and
Miska Petersham. New York, Macmillan Co. [1949]
[32] p.   col. illus.   26 cm.
I. Petersham, Miska, 1888 – 1960, joint author. II. Title.
Full name: Maud Sylvia (Fuller) Petersham.
PZ10.3.P319Bo   49 – 11325*
ISBN 0-02-771350-4

Under a tree in the garden stood a
strange looking box with red wheels.

The gate leading into the garden was wide open.

The curious animals marched through the open gate and walked straight up to the box to find out what it was.

First the cow looked in.
She looked and she looked.
"Moo! Moo!" she called.

"What's this?
Moo-oo-oo-oo-oo-oo!"

Next came the little fat pony
and he looked down into the box.

But then he shook his head.
He didn't know.

Up hopped a rabbit. Hoppity Hop.
He jumped so high that he flopped
right into the box.

Then out he jumped.
He did not know what it was, in that
box with the bright red wheels.

Mother Duck waddled up with her four little ducks.
She stretched out her long neck until she could see.
"Shush! —   Quack, Quack!"
she said to her four ducklings.
"S-H-U-S-H!
Whatever it is, it is sleeping.
Quack, Quack,
Q-U-A-C-K!"

"Meow! Meow! Meow! Meow! Let me look!"
cried the fuzzy black kitten.
And she climbed up and peeked over the edge.
But all she said was, "Purr! Purr! Purr-r-r-r!"
Then around and around the box she walked,
purring softly.

A little dog with long curly ears
came running into the garden.
"Bow Wow! What's all the fuss?"
he barked.

He looked very wise. He knew,
so he sat down close beside the box.

Suddenly up out of the box,
popped — a little round head.

It was a baby.

"Mama! Mama!" the baby called.

"What's this?

And what's this?"

And the curious baby looked from one friendly animal to the other.

Mother came running from the house.
She waved her apron and she shouted
"Shoo! Shoo! Shoo!

S-H-O-O!"

All the animals ran out of the garden.

Mother carefully closed the gate.

The animals were very, very sad.
They wanted to play with the baby.

Mother looked at the sad baby.
She looked at the very,
                    very,
                        very sad animals.

            and then——

Quickly she opened the gate and let them
all come into the garden again.

The gentle

The friendly

The shy

The purring

The with the curly ears

Mother

and her four little

All played together with that baby in the garden.